A NOTE TO PARENTS

When your children are ready to "step into reading," giving them the right books is as crucial as giving them the right food to eat. **Step into Reading Books** present exciting stories and information reinforced with lively, colorful illustrations that make learning to read fun, satisfying, and worthwhile. They are priced so that acquiring an entire library of them is affordable. And they are beginning readers with a difference—they're written on five levels.

Early Step into Reading Books are designed for brand-new readers, with large type and only one or two lines of very simple text per page. **Step 1 Books** feature the same easy-to-read type as the Early Step into Reading Books, but with more words per page. **Step 2 Books** are both longer and slightly more difficult, while **Step 3 Books** introduce readers to paragraphs and fully developed plot lines. **Step 4 Books** offer exciting nonfiction for the increasingly independent reader.

The grade levels assigned to the five steps—preschool through kindergarten for the Early Books, preschool through grade 1 for Step 1, grades 1 through 3 for Step 2, grades 2 through 3 for Step 3, and grades 2 through 4 for Step 4—are intended only as guides. Some children move through all five steps very rapidly; others climb the steps over a period of several years. Either way, these books will help your child "step into reading" in style!

Copyright © 2000 by Berenstain Enterprises, Inc. All rights reserved under
International and Pan-American Copyright Conventions. Published in the United States
by Random House, Inc., New York, and simultaneously in Canada by Random House
of Canada Limited, Toronto.

www.randomhouse.com/kids   www.berenstainbears.com

Library of Congress Cataloging-in-Publication Data
Berenstain, Stan, 1923–
The Berenstain Bears and the escape of the Bogg Brothers / Stan & Jan Berenstain.
   p.   cm. — (Step into reading. Step 3 book)
SUMMARY: The Bear Detectives get to work when the nasty Bogg Brothers escape from jail
and threaten to plunder the Bearsonian, the biggest museum in Bear Country.
ISBN 0-679-89228-1 (trade) — ISBN 0-679-99228-6 (lib. bdg.)
[1. Bears—Fiction.   2. Museums—Fiction.   3. Mystery and detective stories.]
I. Berenstain, Jan, 1923–   .   II. Title.   III. Series.
PZ7.B4483Beek   2000   [Fic]—dc21   98-54963

Printed in the United States of America   October 2000   10 9 8 7 6 5 4 3 2 1

Step into Reading®

The Berenstain Bears
AND THE
ESCAPE OF THE BOGG BROTHERS

The Berenstains

A Step 3 Book

Random House New York

I'm Brother Bear. One day my partners and I were relaxing in our office in the big hollow tree.

My partners are Sister Bear, Cousin Fred, and Lizzy Bruin. We're the Bear Detectives. We share the hollow tree with our friend Dr. Wise Old Owl, who sometimes helps us with tough cases.

Well, we weren't exactly
relaxing. Fred was sweeping
up a bit. Sister was listening
to her favorite music station.
Lizzy was watching a spider
spin a web.

That's when the music on Sister's favorite station stopped.

"We interrupt this program to bring you the latest news: The Bogg Brothers, Bear Country's most dangerous criminals, have escaped from jail."

"Not again!" I said. "Those Bogg Brothers are a nuisance!"

Most of the citizens of Bear Country were law-abiding. But not the Bogg Brothers.

They lived in a tumble-down shack out in Forbidden Bog. They were mean and nasty. The club-carrying, tobacco-chewing Bogg Brothers broke almost every law on the books.

Not only did they rob and cheat, they also made rude remarks and crossed against the light. And every time the police put them in jail, they escaped and robbed and cheated some more.

There was no doubt about it. This was a case for the Bear Detectives. "Follow me!" I cried.

We headed down the road into town.

"Where are we going?" asked Fred.

"To the bank," I said. "That's where the money is, and that's where the Bogg Brothers will go. They've robbed banks before, and my guess is they'll do it again."

But when we got to the bank, we found a police bear already standing guard.

There were no Bogg Brothers to be seen.

"Now what should we do?" asked Sister.

It was a good question. I thought about it for a long moment. "Follow me!" I cried. "There's another place that has money and other valuables!"

"Where are we going?" asked Lizzy.

"To the mall," I said.

But when we got to the mall, we found a number of police bears already standing guard.

There was no way the Bogg Brothers were going to get in there.

BEAR COUNTRY MALL

POLICE

POLICE

"Where should we go now?" asked
Sister.

I reached deep into my brain for
an answer. "To the place that has
the most valuable things in all
Bear Country. Follow me."

"Where are we going?" asked Lizzy.
"To the Bearsonian!" I cried.

The Bearsonian is Bear Country's biggest museum. It has all sorts of valuable things in its collections. It has valuable jewels, valuable coins, valuable fossils, valuable paintings, and all sorts of other valuable things.

The Bearsonian Institution

When we got to the Bearsonian, we found nary a police bear standing guard. We did find Professor Actual Factual, who was in charge of the museum. But he wasn't standing guard. He was sleeping in a hammock.

The Bearsonian Institution

"Wake up, Professor," I said.
"The Bogg Brothers have
escaped from jail. We think they
have come to rob the museum."

"What makes you think that?" asked
the professor.

"This trail of tobacco juice leading to
the museum door," said Sister.

"Where should we look first?" I asked.

"The Hall of Jewels," said the
professor.

The Hall of Jewels was full of
priceless gems.
"Is there anything missing?"
asked Fred when we got there.

"Hmm…now, let me see, let me see," said the professor.

One of the glass cases was empty.

"Yes! Lord Grizzly's great diamond stickpin is missing. Oh, dear! Oh, dear! What should we do?" said the professor.

LORD GRIZZLY'S DIAMOND STICKPIN

"Just follow the tobacco juice," said Lizzy. It led to the Hall of Coins.

We looked around at the cases of old coins.

"Is anything missing?" asked Fred.

LIBERTY PENNY

ANCIENT BEAR GOLD COIN

EARLY SILVER COIN

One of the cases was smashed
and broken.

"It's missing!" cried the professor.
"Bear Country's first-minted coin is
missing! It's priceless!"

The tobacco juice trail led us to the Hall of Fossils.

"Is anything missing here?" asked Fred. The professor looked at his prize Tyrannosaurus rex skeleton. Sure enough, one of the leg bones was missing. The professor was beside himself with grief. "Oh, dear! Oh, dear! My precious collections!" he cried.

QUEEN
ELIZABEAR

B... THE PIRATE

"What's this next room?" I asked, following the trail of tobacco juice.

"The Hall of Wax," said the professor. "It contains wax statues of all the famous bears in history. There're Queen Elizabear, Blackbear the pirate, Attila the Bruin, and many, many others. They're very valuable!"

"Is anything missing?" asked Fred.

The professor looked around at the wax figures.

"No," said the professor. "Nothing is missing—absolutely nothing!"

But that wasn't exactly true. Something was missing.

"Look!" said Lizzy, pointing at the floor.

The tobacco juice was missing. We had come to the end of the trail.

We were very worried. We looked all around at the spooky figures of wax. We were sure the Bogg Brothers were close by... but where?

"We could use some help," said Sister. "I sure wish Dr. Wise Old Owl was here."

"But I am!" Dr. Wise Old Owl *was* there. He was sitting atop Queen Elizabear's crown. He blinked and ruffled his feathers, and this is what he said:

"Is there anything missing?" I heard you ask. But finding what's missing is not quite the task. Your question *should* be, how many more statues are here than there were before?

38

"Hmm, how many more statues are here than there were before?" said Fred in a puzzled voice. The professor had already started counting.

"Eleven, twelve, thirteen, fourteen…"

QUEEN ELIZABEAR

BLACKBEAR THE

R HICKOK

SIR W   BEAR

"That's it!" he cried. "There were twelve before— now there are fifteen!"

The extra three were the Bogg Brothers pretending to be statues.

BEARTHOVEN

DUKE OF BEARING

GENGHIS BEAR

Luckily, the professor had called the police. They arrived in squad cars and stormed the Hall of Wax.

"Hold it right there, Bogg Brothers!" shouted Chief Bruno through a bullhorn.

GENGHIS BEAR

The Bogg Brothers didn't put up much of a fight because they were sick from swallowing tobacco juice. They couldn't spit it out while they were pretending to be statues.

The police led them away.

It didn't take long for the police to find the stolen things. They were hidden in a broom closet.

Chief Bruno had a question. "Just how did you manage to break the case?" he asked.

"Just good old-fashioned detective work," I said.

Then we headed back to our office
to wait for our next case.